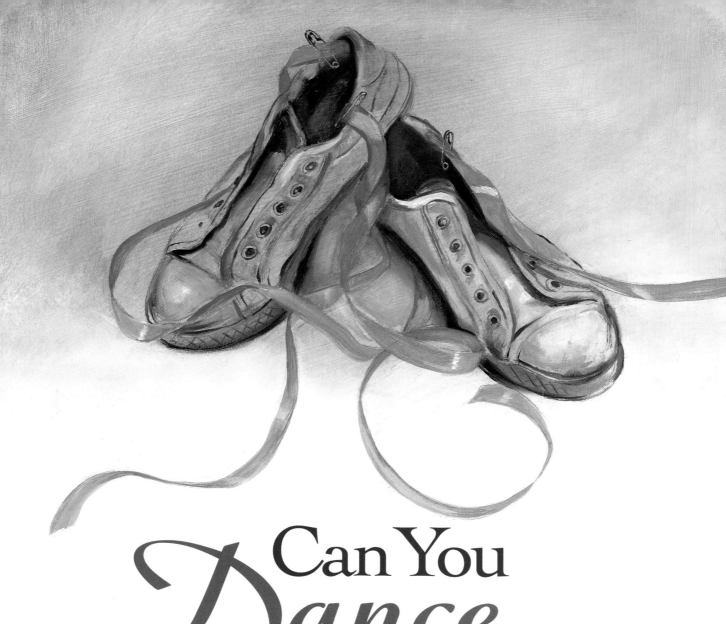

Can You Dance, Dalila?

story by Virginia Kroll

pictures by Nancy Carpenter

Simon & Schuster Books for Young Readers

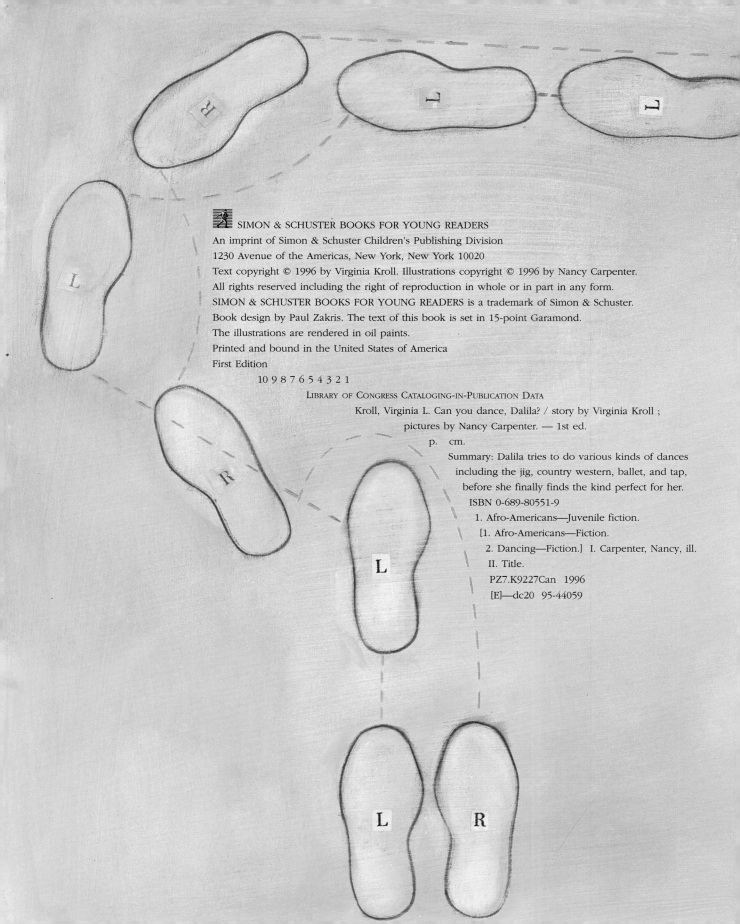

SIMON & SCHUSTER BOOKS FOR YOUNG READERS

An imprint of Simon & Schuster Children's Publishing Division

1230 Avenue of the Americas, New York, New York 10020

Text copyright © 1996 by Virginia Kroll. Illustrations copyright © 1996 by Nancy Carpenter.

SIMON & SCHUSTER BOOKS FOR YOUNG READERS is a trademark of Simon & Schuster.

Book design by Paul Zakris. The text of this book is set in 15-point Garamond.

The illustrations are rendered in oil paints.

Printed and bound in the United States of America

First Edition

10 9 8 7 6 5 4 3 2 1

LIBRARY OF CONGRESS CATALOGING-IN-PUBLICATION DATA

Kroll, Virginia L. Can you dance, Dalila? / story by Virginia Kroll ;

pictures by Nancy Carpenter. — 1st ed.

p. cm.

Summary: Dalila tries to do various kinds of dances
including the jig, country western, ballet, and tap,
before she finally finds the kind perfect for her.

ISBN 0-689-80551-9

1. Afro-Americans—Juvenile fiction.

[1. Afro-Americans—Fiction.

2. Dancing—Fiction.] I. Carpenter, Nancy, ill.

II. Title.

PZ7.K9227Can 1996

[E]—dc20 95-44059

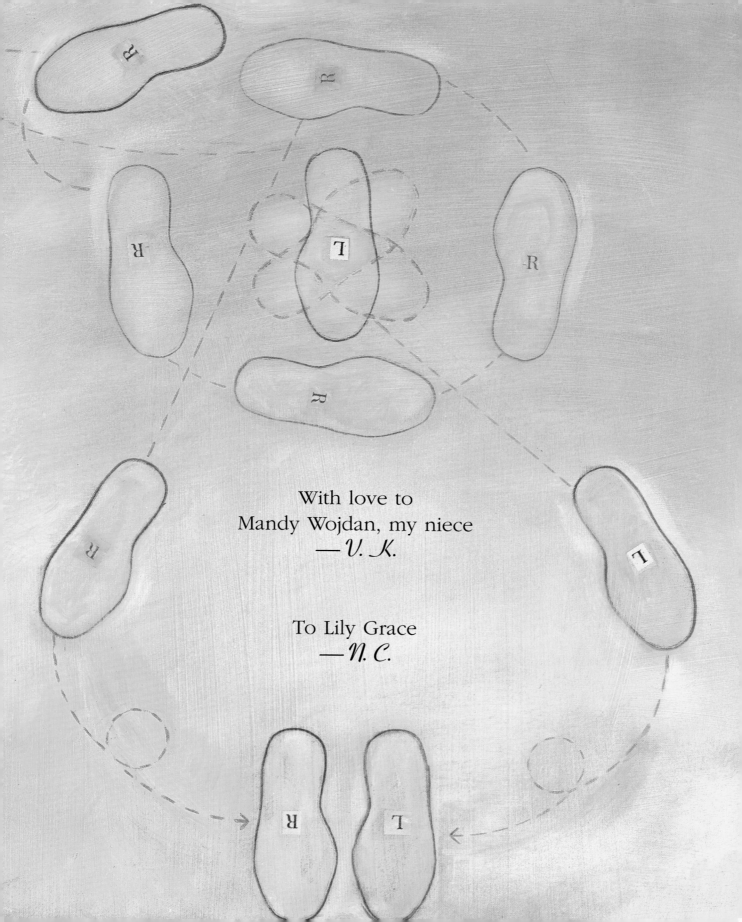

With love to
Mandy Wojdan, my niece
—*V. K.*

To Lily Grace
—*N. C.*

In February, when a fever kept Dalila home from school, Gramma let her watch TV. There was a Valentine's Day special about ballroom dancing.

Dalila watched the partners waltz and tango, rumba and cha-cha. They did promenades and pivots, loop turns and long steps. "Someday I'm gonna dance," Dalila said, falling asleep to a fox-trot.

The next day when she was feeling better, Dalila used Gramma's broom for a partner, but the broom didn't hold her or smile back. And it tripped her when she tried to change places with it.

In March, Gramma took Dalila to the Irish Center where Mrs. Shea's granddaughter Shannon was performing an Irish dance. Dalila watched Shannon's feet move in quick steps and rapid shuffles. Her body was straight and stiff as a pine tree trunk, and she kept her arms rigid at her sides. When Dalila learned that Shannon's dance was called a jig, she giggled. Gramma said, "That's perfect. A neat little name for a tidy little dance."

Dalila went home and put
on her green and white dress.
She tied green yarn to the
ends of her braids. She tried
the jig, but her arms wouldn't
cooperate. They wanted to
keep time with the rest of her.
"There are other kinds of
dancing," said Gramma.

In April, Gramma took Dalila to a line dance demonstration at the community center.

Dalila loved the dancers' western wear and the designs on their leather boots. She liked how they cocked their heads and kicked up their heels, stomped forward, clomped backward, and whooped with their voices now and then. They reminded Dalila of a school of fish, aswish in perfect time.

When Dalila got home, she changed into her jeans and denim shirt and pulled on her winter boots. She asked Gramma to find a country-western radio station, and then Gramma, Dalila, and Dalila's cousin Kiki, who was spending the night, began to line dance, too.

But when Dalila tried to kick up her heels, she bruised her shins instead. And the music kept getting way ahead of Dalila's legs.

"I have a surprise for you," Gramma told
Dalila the last week in May. She held out two
tickets. "Rashida Roberts from church is in the
ballet recital next Saturday."

"Hooray!" Dalila shouted. She had never been
to the Performing Arts Center before.

When Dalila saw the spotlight settle on Rashida, she thought she would never breathe again.

Rashida's skirt was dusted with sequins and rustled like summer leaves. Rashida's arms and legs flowed smoothly, and when she arched her body, Dalila thought of a colorful, sinewy snake curving in one unbroken motion. Rashida leaped across the stage in a grand jeté, and her image whisked by in a glistening blur. "Just like a shooting star," Dalila thought with eyes atwinkle.

Later Dalila put on all four of her swingy skirts and tried ballet in front of Gramma's full-length mirror. "I look more like a frog than a ballerina," she said when she did her first plié. Her feet looked like a clown's when she did tendus. And an arabesque landed her smack on the floor.

At school in June, Jeremy's father came in for show-and-tell. He was the tap teacher at Gotta Dance Academy. He showed the class the clickety cleats on the bottoms of his jet-black shiny shoes.

It seemed that Mr. Wise's feet made three ticks and four tocks for every one step he danced. Sometimes he looked like he was gliding on air, and when he spun, his long arms looked like windmill blades.

Dalila felt the breeze as he whirred past.

Dalila dashed off the bus and headed straight for Gramma's closet. She found Gramma's dressy heels and slid them on.

She scooted to the kitchen and began to brush and shuffle, to toe point and heel drop, just like Mr. Wise showed the class. But her smiles turned to frowns when she listened. Her taps and ticks sounded more like thuds and thumps. At last she stumbled, landing with a bump.

"I'll never be a dancer," Dalila sighed, and she put the shoes away.

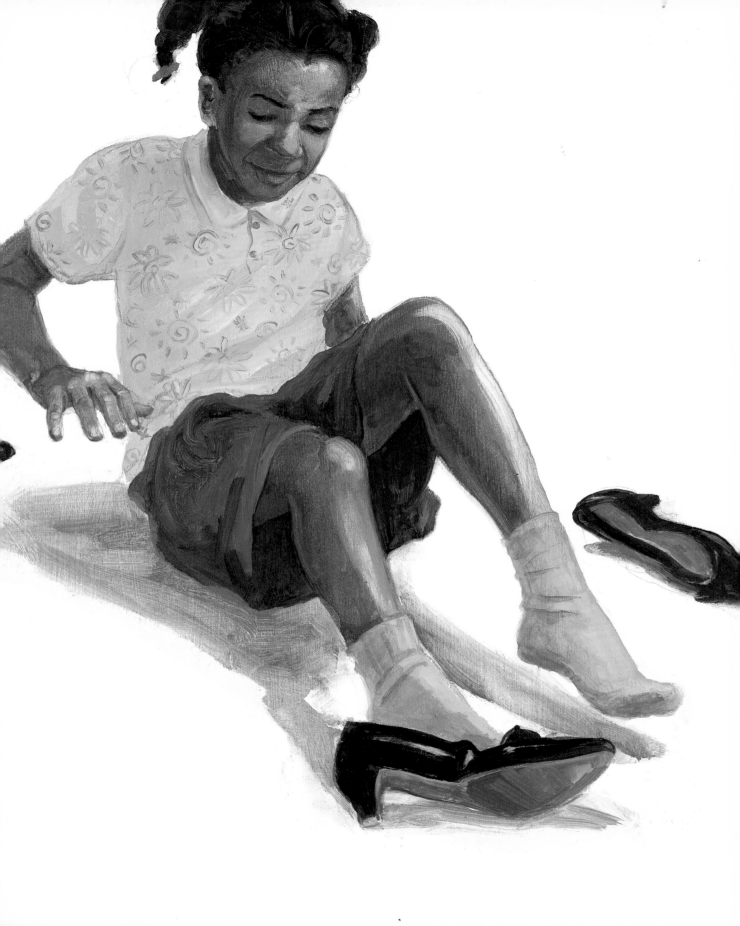

In July Gramma said, "We are going to the festival at the university."

"For what, Gramma?" Dalila asked.

"The West African Troupe is coming," Gramma said.

As soon as Dalila and Gramma got off the bus, Dalila heard the drumming. The noise sent tingles to her tummy and shivers up her spine.

The drums rumbled like thunder. The dancers rocked and reeled to the beat. The rhythm quickened. The dancers bobbed and circled like bushes being blown by a hurricane.

They pranced like young zebras and leaped like antelopes and landed like leopards in practiced pounces. Dalila's hands were sore from clapping.

When there was silence, the
dancers invited the audience to form
an *akpasa*, a group that dances to whatever
feelings the music gives them.

The drums began their beating. And then Dalila
saw no more. She closed her eyes, and her heart was
the drum.

She was the sun-warmed snake, aslither on the
sand. She was the agile antelope and the fish
keeping pace with its partners. She was the
newborn zebra struggling to stand.

Dalila heard galloping hooves all around
her. She opened her eyes. She was the
center of a huge circle. Everyone
was gathered in, caught by the
stirrings of her spirit.

Dalila didn't stop. Her arms and legs were the whirring windmill. Her body was the trembling tree, bowing to the breeze. Most of all, Dalila was the shooting star, dazzlingly bright and lighter than air.